For Bryan Richards,
with all of my best wishes
for success and happiness.

Lucy M. Dobkins
October 27, 1992

DADDY, THERE'S A THERE'S A HIPPO IN THE GRAPES

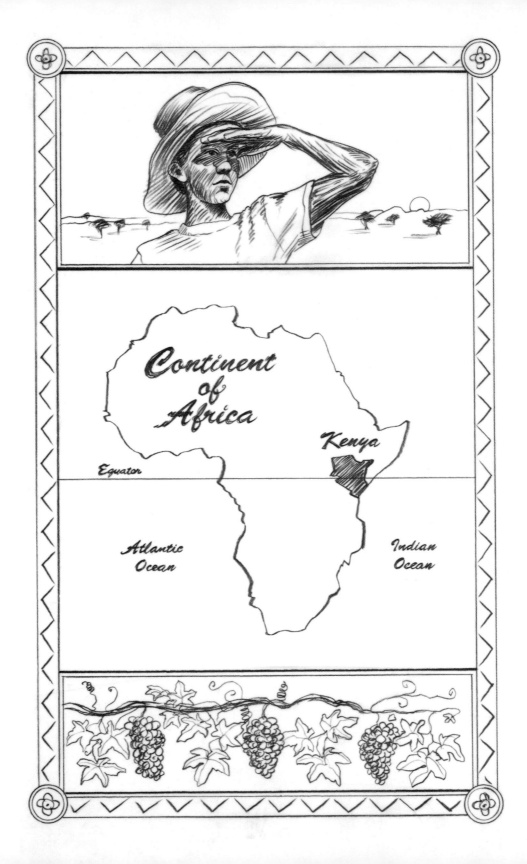

Continent of Africa

Kenya

Equator

Atlantic Ocean

Indian Ocean

DADDY, THERE'S A HIPPO IN THE GRAPES

by Lucy M. Dobkins
Illustrated by Kirk Botero

PELICAN PUBLISHING COMPANY
Gretna 1992

Library of Congress Cataloging-in-Publication Data

Dobkins, Lucy M.
    Daddy, there's a hippo in the grapes / by Lucy M.
Dobkins ; illustrated by Kirk Botero.
        p.   cm.
    Summary: Twelve-year-old Ibrahim, trying to be
responsible, reports to his family that hippos are invading
their Kenya farm, but no one believes him.
    ISBN 0-88289-889-2
    [1. Kenya—Fiction.   2. Hippopotamus—Fiction.
3. Farm life—Fiction.   4. Self-reliance—Fiction.]
I. Botero, Kirk, ill.   II. Title.
PZ7.D657Dad   1992
[Fic]—dc20   92-20321
                                                   CIP
                                                    AC

The word "Pelican" and the depiction of a pelican are
trademarks of Pelican Publishing Company, Inc., and are
registered in the U.S. Patent and Trademark Office.

Manufactured in the United States of America
Published by Pelican Publishing Company, Inc.
1101 Monroe Street, Gretna, Louisiana 70053

*For Tatiana, Lianna, Roxanna, Jeffrey,
and Amy, and for Elmer.*

Contents

DADDY, THERE'S A HIPPO IN THE GRAPES

CHAPTER ONE

What Is Making
That Mysterious Noise?

THUD! DRA-A-A-G. Thud! Dra-a-a-g.

For a moment, Ibrahim Ngobe stopped his task of tying grapevines to the support lines stretching between wooden posts. He stood very still, cocked his head to one side, and listened hard. What was making that noise? Was his father dragging some heavy equipment in the vineyard?

"Is that you, Dad?" he yelled. "I'm over here. Do you want me to help you?"

Nobody answered but there was a shuffling sound.

Ibrahim yelled to his father again. "Is that you, Dad? Here I am."

Thud! Dra-a-a-g.

There it was again. Something heavy was hitting the ground and dragging—sounding closer to Ibrahim each time.

"Dad, are you looking for me? Do you want some help? Where are you?" the boy called once more.

Ibrahim stood perfectly still and listened for his father

to answer him. All he heard was the same mysterious sound.

Thud! Dra-a-a-g.

What could it be? He had never heard anything like it before, and it was coming closer.

Now it was so close that it made the ground shake and the grapevines quiver. Ibrahim felt himself quivering too. It was spooky to work by himself.

Rip!

Ibrahim heard the sound of vines being torn loose from the lines and posts.

C-r-u-n-c-h! Chomp, chomp.

Alarmed, Ibrahim could not imagine what was shaking the ground around him and ripping the grapevines loose from the posts. Whatever was out there was big!

The grapevines grew in long rows that reached all the way to the crest of the hill and down the other side out of sight. Ibrahim looked up the long, green row of vines that were taller than he was. He didn't see anything unusual. He looked down the other way. There was nothing moving in his row, not even the colorful birds that usually perched on the posts and sang their exotic songs. Why was the vineyard so strangely quiet?

Thud! Dra-a-a-g. Rip! Chomp, chomp.

It was utterly silent in the vineyard except for that strange noise coming from the other side of the vines. Ibrahim did not know what it was, but he did know that it was big and it was not his father. What could it be?

Ibrahim bent down on his knees and elbows and lifted the

grapevines so that he could see into the next row. Directly in front of his nose were two large, leathery legs. "What kind of animal is that?" Ibrahim asked himself. "What is this animal in our field?"

He stood without making a sound. Then he stretched up on his tiptoes to try to peer over the top of the vines to get a better look, but the vines were too tall.

"Maybe I can pull apart some vines to make an opening big enough to peek through," he thought out loud as he separated the leaves and tendrils as quietly as possible to open a hole big enough for his head and shoulders.

Ibrahim poked his head through, looked to his left, and saw nothing but long rows of green grapevines under a sunny sky.

When he looked to his right, he almost jumped out of his skin! He was looking directly into a pair of puffy red eyes and a huge snout with bristling black hairs.

The snout and jaws were clamped shut and the upper lip drooped over the lower one. Ibrahim almost laughed. It reminded him of the way his toothless baby brother's mouth smacked shut when he slept.

Then the great, grey jaws opened wide—very wide—and Ibrahim didn't want to laugh any more.

The huge jaws snapped shut around a tall grapevine and easily ripped it off the post as if it were a mere spiderweb. A big hole was torn in the wall of vines—a hole with Ibrahim's head and shoulders right in the middle of it.

"Oh no! It's a hippo!" Ibrahim gasped as the animal's wrinkled head, round body, and leathery legs came into full view.

Ibrahim jerked back so hard and so fast that he fell on his bottom in the row of vines behind him, his arms and legs flailing in the air.

"Dad! Dad! Come here!" he yelled at the top of his voice.

Ibrahim scrambled to his feet and turned to run as fast as he could. He knew plenty of stories about hippos that became angry and dangerous, and he didn't want to be around if this one had a bad disposition.

Frightened, Ibrahim raced up the long row of vines yelling, "Dad! Daddy! There's a hippo in the grapes!"

Mr. Ngobe finally heard him from across the field. "What's wrong, Ibrahim?"

"Daddy, come with me! There's a hippo in the grapes!"

"We've never had hippos in our fields. Have you been day-dreaming in the hot sun?"

"Oh, no! Honest, Daddy, there's a hippo in the grapes! I saw his eyes this close to mine," Ibrahim said as he demonstrated how close they had been.

"I don't see any signs of a hippo. I think you must have imagined it. The heat must have touched your brain. Take a rest this afternoon and come back in the morning when your head is clear," his father instructed.

Angry and hurt that his father didn't believe him, Ibrahim turned toward home. His shoulders slumped and he scruffed his feet in the dust as he walked.

"It's unbelievable," he muttered to himself, "but I know it's true. That huge grey beast, those puffy eyes, the little pointed ears. I can't believe it either, but I know I saw him. I know there really is a hippo in the grapes!"

Ibrahim's mother was surprised and concerned when her

son came home in the middle of the day. "Why are you home so early?" she asked.

"Dad sent me home. I saw a hippo ripping out our grapevines and it scared me. I yelled for Dad, but he said that we don't have hippos on our farm. He thought I was making it up."

"If he didn't see a hippo, there wasn't a hippo. You're not to make up stories any more," Mrs. Ngobe scolded and sent Ibrahim to his room.

Ibrahim fumed. "Now both of my parents are angry at me. They're treating me as if I'm five years old instead of twelve. If Dad would work beside me for a day he'd see the hippo for himself. I'm going to show him the hippo's tracks and the vines he ripped out. Then Dad will believe me. He has to believe me! I never want to lie!"

CHAPTER TWO

Two Hundred Hippos in the Grapes

THE NEXT MORNING, Ibrahim was still angry. He jumped out of bed and hurried to eat his breakfast of mkate mayai—a soft, thin bread wrapped around fried eggs and minced meat. His mother gave him hot chai, which is tea, and he quickly gulped it down. As soon as he finished, he left the table and went outside.

He felt better in the open air and raced to the vineyard. He timed himself, as he usually did, and ran faster than ever before. "Someday, when I've trained enough, I'll run in the Olympics like my uncle," he panted. "Until then, I'll race the stopwatch every day."

"These vines grow like weeds," he declared as he began to tie the new tendrils to the lines. When he helped his father and the other men plant the first grape stocks, they looked like dry, dead sticks. Now they were leafy walls of vines so thick and tall that he could not see through or over them.

"This is a fine day to work," Ibrahim observed in the warm

glow of the morning sunshine. "I'll tie extra vines today to make up for the work I missed yesterday."

Ibrahim whistled and talked to himself as he tied the tender new vines. Morning became afternoon, and the sun burned Ibrahim's shoulders a deeper brown. When the cooler air of evening arrived and the sun sank low on the horizon, Ibrahim knew his day was nearly over and he should start walking home soon.

Halfway down a row, he stopped to stretch his back. In the hush of evening he heard a noise. "What's that?" he asked. Ibrahim stood dead still and listened. "Uh oh! It sounds like the hippo is here again. I hear his big feet thudding and dragging in the dirt. But there is something else. What's making that other noise?"

Ibrahim strained to listen and watched the vines closely. Then he understood what was happening.

"He's ripping out our grapevines again!" Ibrahim shouted, dismayed.

He looked up and down his row of vines but saw nothing unusual. Quietly and cautiously, Ibrahim tore a hole through the wall of vines and looked through it to the other side.

"Oh, no!" he groaned. This time, two huge, grey hippos with sagging jowls were grazing on the grape leaves and tendrils.

Ibrahim did not wait to find out what was going to happen. He did not yell for help, but he did take off running for home—away from the big-snouted beasts.

He raced through the vineyard, out the end of the row, and across the farmyard where chickens pecking in the dirt flapped their wings and scattered out of his way. Ibrahim ran into the house, breathing hard and knees shaking.

Ibrahim's mother was preparing the evening meal and looked up, startled to see her son burst into the house. Mr. Ngobe sat at the table working on farm records. He jumped up and scolded his son for being so boisterous and rude.

"Ibrahim! Quiet! What is the meaning of this, bursting into the house like a crazy boy?" his father demanded.

His heart pounding, the boy held on to the back of a chair. He was out of breath and his chest heaved.

"Daddy, you've got to believe me 'cause it really is true! We have hippos in our vineyard—today there are two!"

"Nonsense. You fell asleep in the sun again. There are no hippos on our land," his father scolded. "Go wash your hands and come to the table."

"Yes sir," Ibrahim said with shoulders drooped, face solemn, and spirit crushed. It was clear that his father did not believe him yesterday and did not believe him today either.

Throughout supper, Ibrahim's mother and father gave him doubtful looks. Ibrahim finished eating and stood up to leave the table. He heard his mother say softly to her husband, "I think it's a stage he's going through."

As Ibrahim left the room, his younger brothers and sisters whispered, "He thinks he saw some hippos, but it was really just a touch of sun on his brain and a stage he's going through." They all laughed behind Ibrahim's back—all except his little sister, Wanjiri. She ran after him and grabbed his hand, pulling him to a stop.

"Ibrahim," she said, "don't feel bad. I believe you. I know

you're telling the truth. There really are hippos in the grapes. I saw two hundred of them myself."

Ibrahim grinned at the pretty child who tagged along almost everywhere he went. He bent over, picked her up, and raised her high off the floor.

"Thank you, Wanjiri. Thank you for believing me. I'm glad you saw the hippos in the grapes—all two hundred of them."

Wanjiri smacked a wet kiss on Ibrahim's cheek and wiggled out of his arms. "Tomorrow, we'll bring a hippo home and show everyone," she said as she ran back to the table.

Ibrahim turned toward his bedroom. "How could they say it was a touch of sun or a stage I'm going through?" he protested, not loud enough for his father or mother to hear. "There were two hippos—real, live, gigantic hippos—ripping out our grapes. I saw them, I heard them, and I know they were there. I think everybody is being unfair."

It was bad enough that his own family didn't believe he was telling the truth, but he worried about what the workmen on the farm would think. Would they say that Mr. Ngobe's oldest son was a liar? That he lived in a fantasy? That he was not reliable enough to work in the fields? Would they lose respect for his father as well as for him? Would everybody laugh behind his back?

CHAPTER THREE

No One Will Ever Laugh Behind My Back!

FOR A LONG TIME that night, Ibrahim lay awake and thought about his family and the farm they owned in the Central Highlands of Kenya, near the equator in Eastern Africa. All his life, he had listened to the history of the family farm.

His grandfather's great-grandfather cleared this land two hundred years ago. Throughout the generations, each father and his sons worked the soil and planted crops. They raised tall corn, hardy beans, golden melons, mangoes, and Macadamia nuts. The soil was rich, and the frequent rain kept the crops lush and green.

Although snow-capped Mt. Kenya could be seen in the distance, Ibrahim never had to wear a coat in this land of bright sun and warm weather. Ibrahim's grandfather called the mountain "the place of brightness." He said it was the favorite resting place of Ngai, their god. Ibrahim wanted to climb Mt. Kenya someday.

The Ngobes' land was close enough to the tropical forests

21

and lakes that Ibrahim's parents once took the children by jeep to see the animals and birds.

The animals and birds came to the Ngobes' farm, too. Sometimes, in the evenings, when Ibrahim walked through the fields inspecting the crops with his father, they saw elephants and buffalo that wandered off the heights. They also heard monkeys chattering in treetops on the ridges of the highlands as sunset turned the sky to red and gold.

Ibrahim liked living on the farm. There were animals to take care of and crops to raise. During vacation from the government school he attended, Ibrahim worked beside the men in the fields. He was the owner's oldest son and was proud to have responsibilities.

One morning a couple of years ago, as the Ngobe family sat down for their breakfast of mkate mayai and hot chai, Mr. Ngobe made an announcement.

"Ibrahim," his father said, "we're going to change our crops. The government of Kenya says the country needs to produce more grapes. We're going to clear off some of our older crops and establish a vineyard. We'll go to the forest and cut eucalyptus limbs for posts and set them in rows in the field. Next, we'll string long lines on them to support the grapevines. Then we'll plant grape stocks. It will be a lot of work, and I'll need you to help."

For weeks, the men and Ibrahim worked in the fields, clearing the old crops and preparing the land for grapes. They went to the forest and cut posts, dug holes for them, and stretched the lines for the vines to climb.

When the fields were ready, Mr. Ngobe showed Ibrahim and the men how to plant the grape stocks. When they finished planting them, the rows of grapevines stretched up the field and over the top of the ridge.

"Every day we'll watch the grapevines," Mr. Ngobe said to Ibrahim. "They'll grow fast. I want you to be responsible for tying the new tendrils to the posts and lines so they will grow upward and be exposed to the sun. This section of the vineyard will be yours to take care of, but I will help you when I have time."

Ibrahim knew it was an honor to be given the responsibility. He was proud and happy, and promised his father he would do a good job.

Now it was two years later. Ibrahim lay in bed unable to sleep. He was troubled that his father no longer trusted him. How was he going to prove that he was a truthful and responsible son? There must be some way.

Ibrahim finally fell asleep, but his dreams were of hippos tearing out grapevines and no one believing what he said.

Early the next morning, not yet fully awake, Ibrahim heard his father shout to him.

"Ibrahim! Get up, Ibrahim! Come and help. I was out in the vineyard before sunrise and there's a hippo in the grapes!"

Ibrahim thought he was dreaming. As he awakened, he wondered if he had heard his father correctly. Did his father actually see a hippo in the grapes? Would be believe Ibrahim now?

"Ibrahim! Get up!" Mr. Ngobe shouted again and shook the boy's shoulder.

Ibrahim jumped out of bed and into his work clothes. He and his father ran out to the truck where the farm's foreman, Nikadi, waited and anxiously looked toward the vineyard.

Mr. Ngobe leaped into the front passenger seat, and Ibrahim jumped into the back. Mrs. Ngobe watched with alarm from the door of the house.

"Drive as close as you can get to the row where I saw the hippo and blow the horn at that ugly beast," Mr. Ngobe directed Nikadi. "Maybe we can drive him out." Nikadi shoved the gearshift and the wheels spun in the dirt.

Nikadi drove fast down the lane to the vineyard and the truck rocked along the bumpy ends of the rows.

"Look down each row of grapes and find that beast," Ibrahim's father shouted.

"There! I see him! He's rolling in the vines!" Nikadi exclaimed and pointed straight ahead.

"He's a big one!" Ibrahim's father said. "Be careful now. Don't drive too close. He might become angry and turn on us and attack the truck."

"Look, Dad, there's another one over there. And another. There are three of them. Four! Five! There's a whole herd of them and they're ripping out our grapes," Ibrahim said.

Mr. Ngobe turned to Ibrahim. "You stay in the truck and blow the horn. Nikadi and I will get out and throw clods and yell at the beasts to try to drive them out of the vineyard. We won't have any grapes to sell if the hippos tear out all our vines."

Ibrahim stayed in the truck and blew the horn steadily while Mr. Ngobe and Nikadi picked up clods of dirt—the biggest they could find—and hurled them at the hippos.

The hippos looked up with their red-rimmed eyes at the men throwing clods and yelling. Their ears perked up at the noise of the horn, but they were not afraid of men or trucks, and clods of dirt didn't hurt their tough, wrinkled hides. They continued to rip out the grapevines.

Finally, either the hippos had all they wanted to eat, or maybe they were irritated by the horn and shouts and clods. They snorted loudly and swung their heads from side to side. The sullen beasts glared insolently at the men, then ambled heavily up the row of grapevines and over the ridge.

"If they come here every day, they'll destroy all our vines. They'll tear out the roots and eat the leaves," Mr. Ngobe said to Nikadi and Ibrahim. "I think we should drive over to the National Game Reserve and speak to the warden. Maybe he can tell us how to keep the hippos out."

Ibrahim was so relieved that his father and the foreman saw the hippos, that he stopped thinking his "I told you so" thoughts. He knew the men would not apologize to him because he was just a boy, but they showed new confidence in his reliability by bringing him with them to help drive the hippos out of the vineyard. Better yet, they were including him on the trip to the game reserve. That was just as good as an apology. After all, there had never been hippos on their farm before they started growing grapes, so why should anyone have believed him? Anyway, his father and Nikadi had the entire farm to take care of and couldn't be everywhere at once. They had to rely on Ibrahim to take responsibility for his share of the work.

"Now that they know I was telling the truth," Ibrahim said in relief, "I'm going to prove I am dependable. No one will ever have cause to doubt me or laugh behind my back again."

CHAPTER FOUR

A Difficult Situation

YELLOW DUST ROILED UP from the dry and rough ruts that served as the only route across the plains. It powdered the men and boy in the truck driving toward the animal reserve. Clumps of tall grass and leafy bushes covered the hilly land alongside the ruts.

Suddenly, Nikadi swerved to avoid a rock and the truck spun into the sand. He wrestled with the steering wheel and carefully controlled the accelerator to try to get out of the hazard. Nikadi's driving mishap didn't distract Ibrahim from the scene beside the sandy ruts. His eyes followed the Egyptian vultures slowly circling over the carcass of a freshly killed antelope lying in the waving grass. A lion with a tawny mane stood over the tender animal tearing out chunks of warm flesh.

In the distance, the boy heard hyenas barking and yipping. They would arrive soon and demand their share of the kill. Ibrahim was sad for the young antelope, but he understood the laws of nature. That was the way of life in Africa.

Nikadi freed the truck from the sand and they resumed

their journey. The rough tracks across the plains took them to the dirt road to the game reserve. They would make better speed now.

Ibrahim watched zebras and giraffes grazing in the valley of grass. Acacia trees with lacy leaves were silhouetted against the purple mountains in the distance. A herd of wildebeests thundered from ridge to ridge. The boy had seen them all before, but he felt the same sense of awe and love for this land and the animals each time he saw them.

"We're leaving the highlands and dropping into lower, flatter land now," Ibrahim's father said and pointed ahead. "Do you see the eucalyptus trees with the flocks of birds in them? Watch carefully. We might be able to see some lilac-breasted rollers. Maybe we'll see baboons, too."

The road wound between groves of broad-leafed trees, dense bushes higher than their heads, and grassy meadows.

"Look!" Ibrahim shouted. "There's a colony of Colobus monkeys in the trees. Look at their long, silky fur. Can I take one home for a pet?"

"No, you already have animals at home. Chickens and goats and now hippos. Isn't that enough? Ibrahim, look along the muddy bank of that lake ahead. Do you see those brown logs floating at the edge of the water? Now watch," Mr. Ngobe said.

Quietly and slowly, the logs glided closer to the shore and raised themselves out of the water. "Crocodiles!" Ibrahim whispered. "What are they going to do?"

"They're going to decide there's nothing good to eat and go back to dozing in the sun," Mr. Ngobe said. "We don't have to worry about them if we stay out of reach. Now, farther from shore, do you see those little pointed ears and puffy eyes showing above the surface? You know what they are, don't you?"

As the truck slowed down, Ibrahim saw a large grey head and snout emerge from the lake.

"A hippo!" Ibrahim shouted.

Other hippo heads suddenly emerged. The water was filled with hippos! Some of them were enormous adults and others were small and young. All the hippos watched the men in the truck.

"Those hippos might be the ones eating our grapevines," Mr. Ngobe said. "Our farm is close enough to this lake for them to walk there to eat. Hippos like to stay in the water during the heat of the day and come out to graze during the cooler hours of evening and morning."

Ibrahim turned his attention to the beautiful pink and white flamingos balancing gracefully on their long legs as they picked algae and shellfish from the shallow water at the edge of the lake. Yellow-billed egrets and red-crowned cranes also waded among the water lilies.

"We're in the national park now," Mr. Ngobe said. "The headquarters buildings are in the next clearing. That's where we'll find the animal reserve warden and the rangers."

Nikadi drove slowly into the grassy meadow and stopped at a large, round wooden building with a thatched roof. Ibrahim was sure it was a model of a native house.

Monkeys chattered and swung from limb to limb in the trees around the headquarters. Woodpeckers tapped noisily on tree trunks. Speckled D'Arnauds Barbets flew from bush to bush.

Ibrahim saw something moving behind the bushes. "Dad! What's that?"

"They are cape buffalo," his father said.

A tall man wearing a crisp khaki uniform and a badge came down the steps of the headquarters building. "Hello. I'm Rohio Kupanya, game warden." He reached out his hand to Mr. Ngobe.

Mr. Ngobe shook his hand. "I'm pleased to meet you. I'm Karioki Ngobe. This is my foreman, Nikadi, and my son Ibrahim."

Nikadi and Ibrahim shook hands with the warden.

"We've come to ask for advice," Mr. Ngobe said. "Our farm is not far from here and the hippos are getting into our grapes. They're ripping out the vines and eating the leaves. We're hoping you might be able to tell us what we can do to keep the beasts out."

Mr. Kupanya looked puzzled. "May I ask why you planted your vineyard so close to the lake and the animal reserve? It's natural for hippos to roam away from the lake in search of food."

"This farm has been in our family for many generations. In the beginning, there were no vineyards, but now the government is asking agriculturists to grow more grapes. We have to grow our crops where we own the land," Mr. Ngobe explained.

The warden looked across the clearing toward the hippos in the lake. He folded his arms over his chest and considered the problem.

"This is a difficult situation. You must not do anything to harm the animals because they could become angry and harm you. What do you have that can make enough noise scare them out of your vineyard?" the ranger asked.

"Well, this morning Ibrahim blew the truck horn and Nikadi and I threw dirt clods at the hippos," Mr. Ngobe said.

"Have you tried hiring workers to beat on drums and lids, or rattle cans with rocks in them? Maybe blow horns and whistles and throw firecrackers?" Mr. Kupanya asked.

"No, we haven't tried that. Ibrahim, you know everybody on the neighboring farms. How many workers do you think we can hire for a few days to see if noise will keep the hippos out?" Mr. Ngobe asked.

"If we hire men, women, and some of the older kids we can probably get six or eight. Do you want me to find out?"

His father nodded. "Yes. Tomorrow, I'll send you to the neighbors to arrange for as many workers as they can let us have."

"I'm sorry I can't give you any other ideas," the warden said. "Just be careful, and let me know what happens."

The men shook hands once more. "Good luck," the warden said and he waved as the truck drove away.

CHAPTER FIVE

The Giraffe Calf

DURING THE DRIVE BACK to the farm, Ibrahim was hardly aware of the brilliant tropical birds near the lake, the antelope that bounded across the hills, and the giraffes that grazed on distant treetops. All he could think about was hiring workers and collecting noisemakers to scare the hippos away. There wouldn't be time to go to the neighboring farms today, but tomorrow he would talk with the owners.

It had been a surprise when Ibrahim's father asked for his opinion on how many workers he thought they could hire. It was even more of a surprise to hear his father say that Ibrahim would do the hiring. Did that mean his father believed he was grown up?

"It looks to me as if my father thinks I'm old enough to work in the fields alone and to hire workers from other farms, and to go on business trips with him. I guess I'm too old to call my father 'Daddy' anymore—even when I'm scared. After all, I am bigger than any of my friends in the sixth year of school. One more year and I'll take the examina-

33

tion for secondary school. I'd say I'm close to being a man," Ibrahim tried to convince himself.

By the time Mr. Ngobe, Nikadi, and Ibrahim got home, it was midafternoon. "Take some mandaazi and casava melon to eat and do as much work in the field as you can. Tonight we'll talk about hiring workers," Mr. Ngobe said.

Instead of running as he usually did, Ibrahim walked to the fields as he ate the bread and fruit. The sun was clear and hot. Brilliant butterflies drifted on the air currents. Tropical birds perched on posts and sang across the rows of vines. Ibrahim was very happy.

"Here's where I stopped yesterday. I can easily tie all the vines in this row before dark," the boy said. He began to straighten and tie the fast-growing vines.

It didn't take much thought to tie vines, so Ibrahim's mind was free to roam. He imagined he was really grown up, eighteen, and training to race. His Olympic-winning uncle was coaching him several hours a day. Ibrahim imagined that he was ready to enter the greatest race in the world.

Deep in his daydreams, Ibrahim thought he felt a warm huff of air blow across the back of his neck. He saw that the grape leaves were absolutely still. There was no breeze at all. He went on tying vines.

Again there came a huff of warm air, this time in his ear. Ibrahim shook his head. "Hm! That's funny!" he said. He kept tying vines.

Then he felt a coarse, scratchy, wet tongue lick the back of his hair.

"What's going on?" Ibrahim reached up to swat the thing in his hair. He felt something soft and velvety.

Alarmed, Ibrahim jumped. "Get out of my hair!" he yelled and whirled around. His eyes popped open wide in surprise. "A giraffe! A giraffe calf! You're trying to eat my hair!"

The little giraffe with its mule-like ears, furry knobs on top of its head, dark eyes with long lashes, and soft muzzle was reaching over the grapevines.

A wide grin spread across Ibrahim's face. "Look at you. Aren't you a pretty pet," he said to the baby giraffe and reached up to rub her muzzle. A long, slender, blue-black tongue wrapped itself around the boy's hand.

"So now we have a herd of hippos and a giraffe calf eating our grapevines. That's nice. That's really swell. What am I going to do about you?"

Just then, a dark shadow fell across Ibrahim. He looked toward the sky, expecting to see clouds. There were no clouds, but there was a fifteen-foot-tall giraffe. It arched its long neck and lowered its head to study Ibrahim's face.

"Oh! I should have known this baby wouldn't be away from home alone. Are you her mother?" Ibrahim asked the huge giraffe that towered over him and blocked out the sun.

The tall giraffe's legs were as long as Ibrahim's head was high, and its swinging neck was as big as a tree. A tickbird nonchalantly perched on the animal's back. The giraffe cow sniffed Ibrahim's hair, licked his ear with her long, dark tongue, and snorted hot, bad breath in his face. She seemed to think the boy was harmless and not worth eating. She turned to nudge her baby.

Ibrahim tore a hole through the wall of vines and watched the gangly giraffes meander up the row. They snacked on tender grapevines all the way.

"This is getting awfully bad," Ibrahim groaned. "We have a community of hippos and a family of giraffes eating our grapevines. It's dangerous to get close to them, even the babies, and I don't know how to scare them away. They're scaring me more than I'm scaring them. What's worse is that they're destroying our vines and we won't have any grapes to sell if they continue. We have to get help fast!"

CHAPTER SIX

An Important Job

"IBRAHIM, AS SOON AS we finish eating breakfast, I want you to run to the neighboring farms and talk with the owners. The closest farm is Mr. Gandhi's, you know, and the next one belongs to Sir Randal-Smythe," Mr. Ngobe said to his son.

The younger children sat at the table and listened, eyes wide. Ibrahim knew they thought he was going to do something important and they wished they were big enough to work in the fields with the men, ride in the truck to see the game warden, and hire workers for the farm. Ibrahim felt lucky.

Wanjiri crawled onto Ibrahim's lap. "Can I go with you? Can I go see our neighbors too?" she asked.

Ibrahim smoothed his sister's mussed hair. "No, our neighbors live too far away for you to walk. When you get bigger you can go."

"Dad, I don't know how to talk to farm owners. What should I say?" Ibrahim asked his father.

Ibrahim was not at all sure he could do this job. What if the neighbors were too busy to listen to him? What if they thought a kid didn't know anything? What if his father was doing this to test him?

"When you get to each farm, look around for the owners. They'll probably be working close to their houses this early in the morning. They already know you, but shake hands with them and tell them I sent you because I can't get away today to see them myself. Explain our situation, and ask if they can send over some of their workers with noisemakers early on Thursday. We'd like to have them work for at least a week. If the noise keeps the animals out of the vineyard, we'll want to keep the workers until after the grape harvest. If the noise doesn't help, we'll have to think of some other way to keep the animals away."

Ibrahim asked, "What should I say if they ask about danger to their workers?"

"Tell them we won't let the workers get close enough to the animals to be in any danger. They're just going to stand at the edge of the vineyard and make all the noise they can. I think the animals will turn away and go somewhere else to graze."

Ibrahim finished eating while his brothers and sisters watched him with envy. It made him feel terrific. Ibrahim's chest swelled and he held his head high with pride. This was his first big chance to show how well he could follow his father's orders.

Farmhouses were rather far apart even though the properties were side by side. Ibrahim took his stopwatch with him and used the opportunity to practice his racing.

He enjoyed the fresh air and the blue sky as he ran past fields of sisal and hillsides of coffee and tea bushes. There were small fields where sugarcane, wheat, potatoes, corn, and beans grew in straight rows.

The first farmhouse Ibrahim came to belonged to Moraji Gandhi. He knew that Mr. Gandhi and his bride had come from India many years ago. They had worked from sunrise to sunset to tame their twenty hectares of wild land and develop them into a productive farm.

The Gandhis had two daughters who went to the same school Ibrahim attended. One of them, Shellina, was in his standard. She was a fine student, good-natured, and so pretty that Ibrahim had trouble keeping his eyes on his books. Maybe he would get to see her this morning. He hoped so.

Ibrahim turned into the farmyard and slowed to a dignified walk. A bamboo thicket surrounded the house on three sides, and banana trees with wide, waving leaves grew near the front door. Chickens and goats roamed in the yard.

Mr. Gandhi, a small and wiry man, saw the boy approaching and waved to him. "Good morning, Ibrahim. What brings you here this early in the day?"

Mr. Gandhi handed a wrench to the man working with him to repair a plow.

"My father asked me to come in his place. He can't get away from the farm today, but he said to tell you he would see you at the first opportunity," Ibrahim said. "We're having a problem with hippos and giraffes getting into our vineyard and tearing out the vines. The warden at the animal reserve suggested we use drums, tin cans with rocks, lids, horns, and firecrackers around the edge of the field to scare away the animals. Do you have any people we can hire for a week to see if that will work?"

Mr. Gandhi hesitated a moment. "We can let you have two women and one man, but only for a week. We'll start harvesting soon and we'll need everyone here. When do you want them?"

"If they can come to our farm early Thursday morning, we'll be grateful. My father said to ask you if the usual pay rate is all right," Ibrahim said.

"Tell your father that's fine. I hope the noise will keep the animals away."

Ibrahim tried to think of something else to say so he could hang around a little longer, but he couldn't think of any way to ask for Shellina to come out of the house.

Mr. Gandhi turned to the plow and tightened a bolt on one of the plowshares. Ibrahim was expected to leave.

"Thanks, Mr. Gandhi. Thanks a lot," he said. He took the stopwatch out of his pocket and began to run.

Ibrahim loped along the dirt road at a comfortable pace. This was a good chance for him to increase his endurance. He would work on his speed later.

The next farm was one of the largest in the highlands. It was about one hundred hectares of coffee and cattle owned by Sir Randal-Smythe. Ibrahim had been inside the large stone house with the cool verandahs once before. All of the furniture was imported from England. The china cabinets were filled with cut crystal and bone china, and sterling silver candle holders gleamed on the white linen tablecloth that covered the long dining table.

Mrs. Randal-Smythe had served tea that day while her pale, delicate daughter, Elizabeth, played sonatas on the polished piano. There were rumors that the Randal-Smythes were related to the royal family in England. This was easy for Ibrahim to believe.

Bougainvillea vines with brilliant blossoms climbed the cool verandahs. White gardenias filled the air with their rich fragrance, and red geraniums grew as high as Ibrahim's chest.

Ibrahim climbed the steps to the front door and knocked. A maid opened the door, but before she could ask the boy what he wanted, Sir Randal-Smythe appeared behind her.

"Good morning, Ibrahim," he said in his deep, loud voice. The tall, strong man towered over the boy. He stretched his hand forward.

Ibrahim reached up to shake his hand and was pulled into the elegant living room. Ibrahim was overwhelmed by the beauty and wealth, and by Sir Randal-Smythe, a banker as well as a farmer.

Ibrahim explained the problem of animals in the vineyard and relayed his father's request for help.

"Yes, I think we can give you a hand," Sir Randal-Smythe said. "In fact, I'll come over myself and take a look at the situation early tomorrow. If it's only for a few days, we can probably lend you seven or eight people. How does that sound to you?"

Ibrahim was impressed with his neighbor's generosity and thanked him for his help. The boy was relieved that he had been able to hire the number of workers his father wanted. His father had given him a job to do and Ibrahim had done it. He felt great, and couldn't wait to run home and tell his father they were prepared to scare the animals away. His father was sure to be proud of him now.

CHAPTER SEVEN

Hairy Thieves

"Ibrahim, you did well," his father said and laid his big hand on the boy's shoulder. "When the workers get here Thursday, I want you to be in charge. You and I will work out the plans ahead of time and all you'll have to do is carry them out. Do you think you can do that?"

Ibrahim was too surprised to speak and merely nodded his head that he understood. Imagine being a sort of foreman!

"Now I want you to go to the vineyard and work on the vines for the rest of the day. You'll need to take some bread and fruit. I'll see you at home tonight," Mr. Ngobe told the boy.

All the way to the vineyard, Ibrahim worried about how to supervise the workers and keep the animals out of the vineyard. Nikadi was foreman for the entire farm and didn't seem to have any trouble, but he was a man and had years of experience. How had he learned what to do? The whole idea was scary.

The sunshine on the vines helped Ibrahim relax and he began to whistle as he tied the vines. They were wet with sparkling drops of moisture from a short rain in the night. Speckled grey and brown birds and brilliant butterflies splashed in the cool raindrops.

Then, thud! Dra-a-a-g.

Ibrahim heard the sound and stopped working. He listened intently.

Thud! Dra-a-a-g.

"So you're back, are you? Well I know all about you. You just hang around for another day, Mr. Hippo, and we'll have a surprise for you," Ibrahim said.

Thud! Dra-a-a-g. Rip! Chomp, chomp.

"Just you wait!" Ibrahim threatened and resumed working with the vines.

After a while, the hippo wandered away chewing a vine. Ibrahim became thirsty working in the sunshine, so he walked back to the end of the row to get the waterbag he'd hung on a post. It wasn't hanging where he had left it. Instead, a long-haired, beautiful black and white monkey sat on top of the post, holding the waterbag in his hands. The monkey had unscrewed the top and was dipping his fingers into the bag and then licking the water off his fingers.

"You rascal! Leave that alone!" Ibrahim yelled. He waved his arms at the hairy thief. "That's my water!"

The monkey jumped in alarm and clutched the waterbag tightly to his chest. He made an irritated croaking sound, leaped from the post to the ground, and sprinted to a post farther away. He scrambled up the post and perched on top, where he could watch the boy yelling and waving.

Ibrahim really wanted that waterbag. It was a hot day and he was thirsty, but he couldn't stop laughing at how clever the monkey was. Now, as he watched the silky little animal, he noticed other monkeys perched on all the posts. They chattered noisily at Ibrahim.

"Don't you scold me, you furry scamps. I'm not the one who stole," he yelled at them, but he wasn't angry. "Maybe I can't have any of you for a pet, but you can't have my water or our grapes either. Now shoo! Go home!"

The monkey with the waterbag just continued dipping his fingers into the water and licking them. The others watched. Ibrahim sighed in exasperation and went back to work, although he was still very thirsty.

"Oh, well," he said. "They might as well enjoy it while they can."

At the upper end of the row, late in the day, Ibrahim reached up to the highest line to tie the last tendrils. Hanging over the top of the vines were the familiar velvety knobs, twitching ears, and big, brown eyes of the baby giraffe.

"You're back, are you? Do you think these tender shoots are pretty good? Did you bring your long-necked mother with you?" Ibrahim said to the baby.

Sure enough, watching from a nearby row were the giraffe cow and bull with green grape tendrils trailing from their jaws.

"Your necks are so powerful you could knock me to the moon if you thought I was going to hurt your baby—but I'm not. I'm not going to hurt any of you, and I don't think you're going to hurt me. I just wish you'd stop eating our vines," Ibrahim said to the bold giraffes. "I can't make you leave, but my work is finished for this evening so I'm ready to go home. I hope you go home too—wherever that is."

"I'll be glad when our extra workers get here. This is more than I can handle," Ibrahim said aloud. "Why did all these animals decide our farm was the place to graze? Other farms have delicious crops too. I sure hope the noisemakers help get rid of these animals before it's too late."

This time, Ibrahim was too tired to run home. He thought he was even too tired to walk. He was beginning to feel sorry for himself. "Why can't I just be a little kid again? I'd like to have just one day to sleep late, play, eat all I want, and take a nap in the afternoon. Why did I ever think I wanted to be grown up? It's hardly any fun at all, and it's going to be worse when I have to supervise the hired help."

Ibrahim turned toward home and began the long walk.

CHAPTER EIGHT

The Fastest Runner in the World

IBRAHIM THOUGHT ABOUT his job: working from sunrise to sunset, running to the neighbors' farms to hire workers, reporting to his father, and working at the far side of the vineyard all day under a hot sun.

He was very hungry and very tired. Every muscle ached. He forgot that, only a few hours ago, he was proud of the responsibilities that his father gave him.

Suddenly, dark clouds hid the late afternoon sun. Ibrahim studied the sky anxiously as large, chilly raindrops splattered on the broad grape leaves and dripped off the tips.

"Why does it have to rain right now? Can't it wait till I get home?" Ibrahim asked in disgust.

The rain fell so hard that Ibrahim was soon quite wet and chilled. His drenched cotton shirt and khaki shorts stuck to his wet skin. His wide-brimmed hat sagged around his ears and water trickled down the back of his neck. He kept his

head down and watched the mud squish around his feet as he sloshed through the field.

Darkness came early and Ibrahim could barely see the outlines of his house and the animal sheds as he neared the farmyard. He didn't feel like it, but he knew he had to do his chores.

Ibrahim was glad to find the chickens and goats already in their pens and out of the rain. At least he didn't have to chase them this time.

"I sure wish you'd feed yourselves and lock yourselves in," Ibrahim said to the goats that butted him in their rush to reach the grain he carried. "I wish you could talk, too. There's never anybody to talk to except myself. Why can't there be somebody my age around here to talk to and someone to run with me? It gets lonely on this big farm. When I grow up and have kids, they aren't going to spend all their time working and talking to themselves."

Lonely, soaked, and cold, Ibrahim fed the goats and chickens and locked their pens. He trudged toward the warm glow of light coming from the kitchen door. The fragrance of corn and chickens roasting on his mother's stove smelled so good that his empty stomach cramped in anticipation.

Ibrahim's mother, her face flushed from the heat of the stove, looked up from the cookpots when the soaked boy walked into the kitchen. "Where have you been so long? We were worried. Are you all right?" she asked. "Get out of those wet clothes and come to the table. Everybody's waiting for you."

"Did you feed the animals?" Ibrahim's father asked. "Are the pens closed?"

Ibrahim nodded. He was tired, and he was tired of being asked every night if he had done his chores. Didn't he always do them? Even when he didn't feel like it? Why couldn't his father just trust him? And why didn't the other kids do more of the work around here? When he was their age, he had plenty of work to do. They were going to grow up spoiled and lazy if his parents were not careful.

The five younger children scrambled to the table. Ibrahim shuffled to his place and slumped in his chair. There were many things to tell his father about the animals in the vineyard, and Ibrahim knew that if he spoke about them, even his brothers and sisters would be absolutely quiet and listen. But he was not in the mood. He was too tired.

Ibrahim took a large helping of chicken and two ears of corn. He ate quickly and silently. The squirmy little kids got on his nerves. They were so immature! Why couldn't they just be quiet and eat their supper!

Mrs. Ngobe watched her oldest son and worried. It was not like him to gobble his food in silence and not tease the younger children even once. Ibrahim's eyelids drooped and his head nodded sleepily as he chewed.

Mr. Ngobe observed his son's bad mood and fatigue and didn't ask him about his day's work. He would let him eat and go to bed. They could talk at breakfast. This would not be the last time Ibrahim would be exhausted and grumpy. Farming was hard work, and the sooner Ibrahim and all the other children knew it, the better.

Ibrahim did not feel much better when he awoke the next morning. His muscles still ached and he did not want to go to work. Why couldn't he ever have a day to sleep? Or play? Other kids did not work as hard as he did. Even Nikadi got one day off every week.

During breakfast, Ibrahim told his father about the animals that were in the vineyard the day before. "I can't keep them out. They're pestering me, and they're tearing the vines. They're even beginning to eat the grapes that are getting ripe. What do you want me to do?" he asked.

Mr. Ngobe said, "You'll get help tomorrow when the workers get here. Today, I want you to work with the vines and keep your eyes open for animals. Don't try to scare them by yourself. If any of them act as if they might hurt you, leave the vineyard and come home. I don't want you injured."

Ibrahim felt a little better.

"Our hope is that noise will keep the animals out of the vineyard and we won't have any more problems this season," Ibrahim's father said.

Ibrahim and his father finished eating their hot ugali and drank their chai. The younger children were messy, as usual. How did their mother tolerate it?

Wanjiri watched her big brother until he got up from the table. Then she ran over and hugged him with fingers sticky from pineapples and a ring of milk around her mouth. Wanjiri could make Ibrahim smile even when he didn't want to.

Out in the clear morning air, Ibrahim felt guilty that he was walking to the vineyard instead of running. He knew he ought to practice racing and should get to work as soon as he could, but he was still tired and didn't have the energy.

He entered a row of vines and checked for wild animals.

Maybe there would be so many that he would have to go home. All he saw were flocks of birds that pecked at the clusters of grapes turning ripe.

"We need some scarecrows with arms that flap in the wind," the boy said to a large black bird that wasn't even frightened enough to fly away.

Ibrahim was getting tired of this boring job and he escaped into daydreams again. This time, he was in the Olympic stadium. His feet were the fastest in the world, and his endurance was the greatest. He pounded toward the finish line, two strides ahead of his closest competitor. He reached the finish line and broke the white tape with his heaving chest. The crowd went wild.

Ibrahim, carried away by his imagination, threw his arms over his head in a gesture of victory.

Excited and out of breath, Ibrahim was stunned when something butted his behind so hard that he sprawled face first into the vines.

CHAPTER NINE

Hoofs, Teeth, and a Twitchy Tail

IBRAHIM WAS INSTANTLY shocked back to reality. He untangled himself from the vines and crawled out on his hands and knees. He was at eye level with four black-and-white striped knobby knees and velvety legs.

He raised his eyes from the knobby knees to a horselike chest, a strong neck with a black stubby mane, and the striped head and blinking eyes of a young zebra.

"Did you butt me into the vines?" Ibrahim demanded.

The zebra, ready to bolt in an instant, watched the boy cautiously. Ibrahim didn't move a muscle. "It's not enough that we have hippos and giraffes and monkeys and birds eating our grapes. Now it looks like we have zebras," he said. "Did you wander away from home or is your mother here, too? Maybe your whole neighborhood came over. Did they?"

The sleek little zebra's ears flicked back and forth. His frisky tail swished. He moved one step closer to the boy and sniffed his hair and face.

Ibrahim could hardly keep from reaching out to pet the zebra, and he had to stifle giggles when the zebra tried to take a bite out of his sleeve.

"That's not good to eat. Our grapes are not for you to eat either—even if everybody else seems to think otherwise. Why don't you go find your mother and let me get my work done?" Ibrahim said to the little animal. He looked away from the young zebra and saw a full-grown one coming into the row of grapes, apparently searching for her baby.

"Is that your mother? How about turning around and going to meet her? Then you can trot home together. I have work to do, and I don't need any help from someone with hoofs, sharp teeth, and a twitchy tail. It was nice meeting you, but good-bye!"

The big zebra snorted and tossed her head, suspicious that the boy might hurt her baby. The little zebra tried one last time to take a nip out of Ibrahim's shirt. Then he turned, swished his tail, kicked up his heels, and trotted down the row to nuzzle his mother. Ibrahim watched them until they went around the end of the row and disappeared over the ridge.

It seemed as if all the animals wanted to be there. Was noise in the field going to keep any of them out?

"There are more of them than there are of us, and they probably won't be afraid of the noise of the workers. We can try it, but we better think of some other ideas too. When the grapes are ripe in a few days, we'll have more company— especially monkeys and birds," Ibrahim said aloud. Although there wasn't anyone nearby to hear him, he continued, "I'll do the best I can, but I'll be glad when school starts and I can do something other than worry about grapes."

At the middle of the day, Ibrahim stopped long enough to eat his banana and a somosa. He felt like curling up in the shade of the grapevines and taking a nap, but knew he shouldn't take the time. He needed to finish tying this row of vines today because he would be supervising the hired help during the next week, and wouldn't have time for anything else.

Late in the afternoon, storm clouds boiled over the mountains, crossed the ridges and valleys and settled over the Ngobe farm. Rain poured so heavily that Ibrahim was quickly soaked. His shoes squished. His old hat got so soggy and limp that it would never be the same. Rivulets of water streamed down the rows of vines and formed larger streams at the low end of the field. Dusty soil turned into sticky mud.

Ibrahim's disposition had not been very good at the beginning of the day, and it worsened with the rain. He was wet and miserable. By the time the rainstorm passed, it was time to go home and he did not finish his work.

Trying to wash some of the thick layer of mud off his feet, he sloshed through puddles of water. It didn't do any good because, three steps from the pudddle, the mud was caked as thickly as before. Several times, Ibrahim slipped in the slimy stuff and fell. Mud splashed on his face and in his hair. His clothes were filthy. He was a muddy mess.

By the time Ibrahim slipped and slid all the way home, he was so tired and so mad that all he wanted to do was get clean, eat something hot and go to bed.

He entered the farmyard and looked to see where the

chickens and goats were. Were they soaked too, or warm and dry in their pens? He started toward the goat pen in the dark, and slipped once more in a puddle of gloppy, slimy gook.

That did it! Tired, cold, hungry, wet, and muddy, Ibrahim broke into tears. He sat in the puddle, tears streaming down his face and mud dripping from his ears. It was useless to try to wipe off the tears; all it did was smear the mud around.

Ibrahim couldn't do any more work. The chickens and goats would just have to take care of themselves. They weren't going to starve by missing one meal, and they weren't going to get away on a night like this—even if their pens weren't locked. Were they?

Ibrahim gave up and went to the back door of the house. Mrs. Ngobe's mouth dropped open in astonishment at the mud-covered mess who stood at the door.

"Get those muddy clothes off and leave them outside," she said. "I'll get some water ready and you can clean up. You're shivering. You'll catch cold if you don't get warm."

Ibrahim looked so awful the children stopped their noisy playing and stared at their brother. He noticed the table was set for supper, but his father wasn't there. That was unusual. Where was he?

The wonderful smells of vegetable goatmeat stew and baked bread filled the house. The smell made Ibrahim begin to feel better. He washed off the layers of mud, put on dry clothes and went back to the kitchen.

Ibrahim's father came in the door. He was late, wet, and unsmiling. He spoke to his wife, stood in front of the stove for a few minutes, and went to his seat at the table. The children took their places and their mother brought bowls of stew and fruit, and a basket of hot bread.

Mr. Ngobe turned to Ibrahim and said, "That was a bad storm. It caught me at the south end of the farm and turned the road into such a mud hole that the truck is stuck. We'll have to go back tomorrow and dig it out." As he spooned stew onto his plate, he asked, "Did you feed the chickens and goats and lock the pens before you came in?"

Ibrahim looked down at his plate. Of all nights, why did his father have to ask this time?

His father's eyes bored into him, suddenly suspicious. He waited for an answer.

Ibrahim sat perfectly still, hardly able to breathe. What if he said yes he did? Who was going to check up on him on a night like this? But what if someone did check?

No one spoke. The children sat so still they didn't even lift their spoons. Mrs. Ngobe seemed upset. Mr. Ngobe looked stern. Everyone waited.

Ibrahim raised his eyes and felt hot tears form in them and drip down inside his nose. He looked miserably at his father.

"No, sir. I didn't."

Ibrahim's father looked as if someone had hit him in the stomach. Was he disappointed or angry? Or both?

"I meant to feed them, but it was dark and muddy and I couldn't see. I fell in the mud and I didn't think it would hurt them to miss just one meal," Ibrahim blurted. Why did his father look so sad?

"Ibrahim, it is your job to take care of the chickens and goats. They probably won't starve in one night, but I want you to understand what it's like to go without food. I want you to leave the table now and go to bed."

Ibrahim's mother quietly rose from the table and stood by the stove. The children didn't quite understand what was happening and stayed silent.

"Furthermore, I think it was a mistake to give you more responsibility. Tomorrow, when the workers come, you will not supervise them. Instead, you will work with them, and your station will be the last one at the farthest end of the vineyard. Your job will be to rattle rocks in tin cans. When I believe you are ready for more responsibility, we will talk about it," Ibrahim's father said.

Ibrahim's throat tightened up with a hard knot. Tears poured down his face. Ashamed that he didn't do his chores, and ashamed of crying, he jumped up to leave the table and accidentally pushed his chair back so fast that it turned over and crashed to the floor.

Ibrahim's father leaped up in a rage and towered over the boy. Ibrahim had never seen him so furious.

As fast as he could, Ibrahim picked up the chair, pushed it up to the table, and ran out of the room, his face crumpled up in misery and wet with tears.

CHAPTER TEN

Here's the Plan

SIR RANDAL-SMYTHE'S dusty truck drove slowly into the Ngobe's farmyard and stopped in front of the house. Chickens squawked and scattered. Sleek goats chewed tufts of grass as they watched the men and women leaning over the wooden sideboards of the truck.

"Good morning!" Sir Randal-Smythe boomed in his jolly voice as he dropped down from the cab. "It's a beautiful morning. I brought eight of my people and picked up three at Gandhi's. We have as many noisemakers as we could get."

Mr. Ngobe hurried to shake his neighbor's hand. Ibrahim stood behind him, quiet and subdued.

"Thanks. We appreciate the help. Here's the plan. Your eleven people and Ibrahim will line up along the north side of the vineyard. That's where most of the animals enter. The workers will be able to see any animals that get close. As soon as they see one, they'll bang on the lids, rattle the tin cans, blow the bicycle horns and beat the drums. We think that the noise will alarm the animals and they'll go back to the forest and plains. We don't expect anyone to be in danger, but I'll be nearby and so will my foreman, Nikadi," Mr. Ngobe explained.

"You're probably right. If you need any more noise, I can send some firecrackers with my people tomorrow," Sir Randal-Smythe offered. "If I didn't have to get back to my own place, I'd stay and help. I'll send my man back to pick up these folks at dark."

The workers with their noisemakers jumped out of the truck and waited for orders.

"We're going to walk up this side of the vineyard to the ridge," Mr. Ngobe said and he pointed to the north side of the field. "Space yourselves several hundred meters apart. When a hippo, zebra, monkey or giraffe comes into sight, make as much noise as you can until they turn away. We'll quit at sundown."

Within an hour, workers were in place all along the side of the field. Ibrahim took his position high on the ridge at the far northwest corner of the vineyard. His was the longest walk, but he had the best view. He looked down on rows and rows of dark green vines and the workers who watched the plains for animals.

Throughout the day, whenever an animal approached, the noise began. The racket was obnoxious. It made the animals nervous and they either turned and ran or flicked their ears and paced back and forth in front of the workers.

By the end of the day, Mr. Ngobe was satisfied that the noise was going to keep the animals away. The grapes would ripen without being eaten. There would be a money crop.

The second day was not as easy as the first. The animals became more curious and courageous. Mischievous monkeys slipped between the workers too quickly to be stopped. They feasted on the juicy grapes.

Hippos lumbered heavily along the side of the field looking for an unguarded place. Then, with determination in their reddened eyes and their heads swinging in defiance, they crashed past the workers in spite of the noise. No one dared to try to stop them. They ripped out the vines and trampled them into the dirt. They could do the same to a man.

The zebras were fearless as well. They neither waited nor bothered to go around the workers. They trotted between them without hesitation. If a worker attempted to scare them away, the zebras drew back their lips to show vicious teeth, then kicked their hind legs.

It was not until the third day that Ibrahim saw giraffes on the plains. The beasts were so tall that they could see the noisy workers from far away. They were smart so they galloped to the west end of the field where there were no guards. They went into the field whenever they pleased.

Mr. Ngobe worried about losing the grape crop, and he worried even more about the safety of the workers.

Ibrahim stood on top of the ridge and studied how each of the animals behaved during the long days. They were afraid of neither men nor noise. Everyone soon realized that they had to find another solution to the problem of the animal invaders.

Ibrahim thought about the problem as he rattled his tin cans. He knew that hippos often liked to graze during the cool hours of the night, but there weren't any guards to even try to stop them at those times. Giraffes and zebras were fast and could rush between the guards. They were dangerous too, with their teeth and hoofs. The giraffes' necks were powerful weapons to swing at their enemies. Monkeys were so clever that they could imitate people. They also moved fast and leaped far. What could stop them? How could they keep the animals out of the grapes? There had to be answer.

Ibrahim was accustomed to daydreaming while he worked, but all this activity was too interesting to miss. Now he kept his mind on his work. He watched the animals when they came near the field. He paid attention to the workers and made sure they were in their places and safe.

He kept trying to think of ways to keep the animals out of their fields. They always came from the north, so that side of the vineyard should be closed off somehow. How do the cattlemen keep their livestock penned in? Would the same method work to keep wild animals out? What about the deep ravine on the plains that the animals cannot cross? How could they dig a ravine like that next to the farm? Where could they get labor and heavy equipment?

Ibrahim began to get some ideas. He wondered what his father and Nikadi would think. Should he even talk to them about what he was thinking? What if they thought his ideas were dumb?

CHAPTER ELEVEN

Monkeys with Toothy Smiles

"I HEAR YOU'VE GOT trouble," the stranger shouted as he leaped out of the truck he had just parked in front of the Ngobes' house.

Ibrahim had never seen anyone that big before. The man's shirt stretched over his bulging muscles and thick chest. He was a head taller than Ibrahim's father—and Ibrahim's father was one of the tallest men in the area. Mr. Ngobe strode across the farmyard. "I'm Karioki Ngobe. You must be from Sir Randal-Smythe's farm. This looks like his truck."

"Yes, I'm Mohammed Juma, his foreman. He told me to come over and find out what I can do to help. He sent five extra workers today and Mr. Gandhi sent two."

"We appreciate your help. The animals are out of control. There are so many of them invading the vineyard that we're sure to lose our grape crop for the year. I'm worried about the safety of the workers, too," Mr. Ngobe added. "We'll welcome any suggestions."

"I brought these firecrackers. Let's give them to the workers. They can use their other noisemakers when the animals first appear, and if the animals keep coming, they can light the firecrackers and throw them," Mr. Juma said.

"That might help," Mr. Ngobe agreed. "Now that we have more people to guard the field, we won't be so far apart."

The work crew took their noisemakers and the firecrackers Mr. Juma handed to them. They headed for the field.

Mr. Juma extended his hand to Ibrahim. "Are you Ibrahim, the boy I've heard about?"

Ibrahim didn't know whether to be pleased or not. Had the man heard good things or bad?

"Yes sir, I am," he answered.

"Why don't you take me to the vineyard and show me where you're stationed. I'll take the station next to you," Mr. Juma said.

Ibrahim wondered if that was an honor or if the foreman was here to supervise him and make sure he did his job right? Ibrahim was suspicious, but he led Mr. Juma through the vineyard to the last row on the ridge. Mr. Juma seemed friendly enough and talked about what the highlands were like when he was a boy growing up.

"Life out here is a lot easier than it used to be," he began. "These days, we have comfortable houses and roads from one farm to another. We have better equipment than we used to have as well. We don't have to do all the work by hand anymore, and we don't have to wonder if a lion is going to pounce on us in the fields either. The only animals we worry about now are the ones that try to eat our crops. That's not nearly as bad as worrying about them trying to eat us."

"This is my station," Ibrahim interrupted, and stopped on the top of the ridge.

Mr. Juma looked over the rows of grapes on the hillside, then turned to study the plains.

"This looks like the best place to see all the workers and the animals," Mr. Juma observed. "I'll move down the ridge about a hundred meters or so. Between you and me, we'll see so many animals, and make so much noise that none of them will want to come into your field."

Ibrahim watched the foreman stride down the slope. What long steps! He could win a race just by walking.

The guards were in place at the edge of the vineyard for only a few minutes, when a colony of monkeys scampered toward them. The barrage of noisy drums, shrill whistles, horns and tin cans had no effect on them. The monkeys came closer.

"Throw your firecrackers!" Mr. Juma yelled. "Yell at them. Wave your arms. Scare them away!"

The guards dropped their noisemakers on the ground so they could throw firecrackers. The monkeys waited patiently until the explosions stopped. Then they saw the noisemakers, picked them up, and carried them past the guards and into the vineyard.

A group of monkeys scampered up the wooden posts and perched on top. They sat in the sunshine and beat the drums, rattled the cans and banged lids exactly like the people had done. Their wide lips turned up in toothy smiles. Other monkeys bounced up and down on their hind legs and waved their arms, imitating the amazed guards who now watched them.

As frustrated as they were, Ibrahim and Mr. Juma laughed until they couldn't laugh anymore.

CHAPTER TWELVE

They'll Kill Him!

LARGER ANIMALS BEGAN TO arrive, and the workers turned their attention to them. Never before had so many zebras and giraffes come to the field. They came in herds.

The ugly hippos arrived and paced along the side of the field watching for a space where they could break in.

The guards became nervous about the large number of beasts trying to get to the grapes. They beat their noise-makers frantically. They ran up and down the edge of the field, yelling and waving their arms, but the beasts were not scared. The vineyard was becoming more dangerous by the minute.

Suddenly, from his station high on the ridge, Ibrahim saw an even greater danger! Two enormous hippos were trudging from the center of the vineyard where they had been grazing during the night. They were full and wanted to go back to the lake, but their path was blocked by men and women running, yelling, and beating noisemakers.

The hippos first seemed a little irritated and nervous, and then became obviously angered. They plunged one way and

then another, trying to get out of the field and away from the racket. The heavy beasts soon became so enraged that they lowered their heads ominously and charged full speed toward an open space at the edge of the field. At the very moment the beasts began thundering toward it, Mr. Juma ran into the opening! He was looking the other way and yelling at the animals coming from outside the field. He didn't know there was danger behind him too.

Blocked and crazed by the obstacle in their path, the hippos began mauling the man with their snouts and powerful jaws. They knocked him down and trampled the ground around his head and body. The man threw his arms over his face to protect himself and tried to stand up, but the hippos knocked him down again.

"They'll kill him!" Ibrahim screamed above the noise.

The workers looked up when they heard Ibrahim, but did not see what he was screaming about. Ibrahim raced off the ridge, yelling at the top of his voice, "Help him! The hippos have him!"

Ibrahim still had a few firecrackers in his pocket. He lighted them as fast as he could and tore straight toward the massive, pawing beasts. He threw the firecrackers under their bellies and screamed, "Get away! Get away!"

Now the workers did see the terrible fight, and ran to help. They charged the hippos, yelled, waved their arms, and banged all the noisemakers they had.

The confused hippos hated the commotion and were desperate for a way out. Panicked, they wheeled around and crashed through rows of vines, narrowly missing several workers, and thundered out of the field. Torn grapevines trailed from the hippos' heads and legs as they raced across the plains.

Every worker in the field, out of breath from running, crowded around Mr. Juma. Nikadi arrived and pushed his way through the people surrounding the injured man.

Carefully, Nikadi examined him. He was bruised, and blood flowed from gashes all over his body, but no bones were broken.

"You took a beating, and you're lucky to be alive. Lie still until we stop this bleeding, then we'll put you in the truck and take you home," Nikadi told the limp foreman.

The women from Sir Randal-Smythe's farm pressed cloths on the wounds and held them tightly to stop the bleeding.

It was a while before the battered man's heart stopped pounding and he began to breathe normally. Nikadi looked around for Ibrahim and saw him all alone under a grapevine, watching the women treat the injured man. Nikadi walked over and knelt beside the boy.

"You did a foolish but very courageous thing, Ibrahim. The hippos were crazed and dangerous. You probably saved this man's life," he said. "Your father will be very proud of you."

Ibrahim was grateful for Nikadi's praise. He did want his father to be proud of him, and he remembered the punishment he received when he hadn't done the right thing. The thought of that punishment made Ibrahim think about the hippos who mauled the man, and how he fearlessly rushed to help. If he was courageous, and if his father was going to be proud, would the punishment end?

He wondered about something else too. Maybe Nikadi knew the answer. He asked in sadness mixed with anger,

"Why does my father make me do everything exactly right? Why does he make me work harder than any of the other kids? Why can't he wait for me to grow up?"

Solemnly, kindly, Nikadi answered. "He did. He waited twelve years. Now you are grown up and your father needs you."

CHAPTER THIRTEEN

Ibrahim's First Trip to the City

"IBRAHIM, THIS PLAN ISN'T working," Mr. Ngobe said at breakfast. "I think we should leave Nikadi here to manage the farm for a couple of days, while you and I drive over to the agricultural college. There must be some people there who know how to deal with the animal problem. I know this is not the only farm that's losing crops to wild animals."

Mrs. Ngobe's eyes became moist and shiny. She smiled at Ibrahim, happy the punishment was over.

The other children stopped eating and listened, their spoons halfway to their mouths. They knew something important was happening—even if they didn't understand it.

Ibrahim couldn't hide his surprise and excitement. A two-day trip to a college! Professors and classrooms and laboratories! A chance to learn some of the things he'd need to know in order to farm this land by himself someday. Best of all, his father wanted him to go!

"We'll leave tomorrow after breakfast," his father announced.

Mr. Ngobe turned to the son next in age to Ibrahim. "Jaroni, I want you to be responsible for the goats and chickens from now on. Go with Ibrahim today, and learn what to do. If you have any questions, he can answer them."

Ibrahim tried to act dignified, but he was too happy and excited. He had finally outgrown the goat-and-chicken chores! He nudged his brother in the ribs with his elbow.

"Come on. I'll show you what to do," he said.

Wanjiri slipped out of her chair and followed behind her two brothers. "I want to learn, too. Then, if Jaroni falls in the mud, I can do his chores and nobody will get mad anymore," she said.

Ibrahim picked her up and carried her over his shoulder. "Okay, it won't hurt for Jaroni to have a back-up. We'll teach you all about it."

He set her on the wooden rails of the goat pen and took Jaroni inside. "Here's what you do. . . ." he began. Ibrahim showed his younger brother his new responsibilities and he anxiously awaited the next day's long journey.

Ibrahim had never before traveled so far from the farm. During the four-hour drive to the city in which the agricultural college was located, he gazed at the scenery and wondered if the professors would be able to help them solve their problem.

When they arrived on the college campus, Mr. Ngobe seemed to know exactly where to park. He walked directly to the Professor of Agriculture's office without needing to ask for directions. Ibrahim was surprised that his father was so familiar with a place so far from home.

The secretary promptly took Mr. Ngobe and Ibrahim into the professor's office.

"I'm very pleased to meet you, Mr. Ngobe," the professor said. "Your family is well-known here. You own the large farm close to Sir Randal-Smythe. I know that your family has owned it for over two hundred years. It was your father who first had the idea of establishing this agricultural college and he convinced the government to build it. If I am not mistaken, you were one of the first students to graduate from here."

"Thank you, Dr. Ngwari. Yes, I'm proud to be a graduate of this school. It has helped me in my business," Mr. Ngobe said. "I hope my son will have a chance to attend."

"Is there something I can do for you in the meantime?" the professor asked.

"Yes, there is. Have you had any experience with wild animals invading and destroying farm crops? We planted grapevines on part of our farm, and the beasts seem to prefer them over any other crops. We can't keep the monkeys, hippos, zebras and giraffes out of the vineyard and they're tearing out the vines."

Mr. Ngobe told the professor about how Ibrahim discovered the first animals in the vineyard and described the great numbers of them that came every day since. He described how they hired workers with noisemakers, and how the foreman was injured by hippos.

The professor shook his head. "This is the worst animal

problem I've heard about. I don't know what you can do. Although I doubt anyone else on the faculty knows either, I'll ask."

Mr. Ngobe stood up to shake the professor's hand and leave, but the professor motioned for him to wait.

"Ibrahim has had plenty of opportunities to learn about your wild animals. It sounds as if they get closer to him than anyone else. I'd like to ask if he has any ideas about keeping them out of your field," Professor Ngwari said.

Mr. Ngobe was a little surprised, but he sat down and nodded his head, indicating that it was all right.

The men looked at Ibrahim and waited. Ibrahim's brain locked and so did his mouth. He instantly forgot everything he had learned from watching the wild animals. What could he tell a college professor?

The silence was brief, but to Ibrahim it seemed like hours before he was able to say anything.

"I don't know very much compared to you and my father," Ibrahim began, "but there are a few ideas I've been considering this week while I watched the animals come off the plains to our farm. They almost always approached from the north side and hardly ever went to the east, south or west sides of the farm."

Dr. Ngwari and Mr. Ngobe listened attentively as Ibrahim continued, "What if we dug a deep trench along the north side of the farm? We could ask to borrow workers from our neighbors and repay them with crops. Maybe the government would provide an earth-mover as part of the Program of Assistance for the Protection of Wild Animals—although this is actually protection *from* wild animals instead of *for* them."

The professor's eyes sparkled at the ideas.

The boy added, "The trench would have to be dug with sides steep enough that hippos couldn't climb in and out, and wide enough that giraffes and zebras couldn't jump across. To be sure to stop them, we could build a high thorn fence on the bank of the trench. Thorn fences make good corrals to keep farm animals in, so they probably will keep wild animals out."

Ibrahim paused. Was he talking too much?

"Go on," the professor urged.

Ibrahim looked at his father. His father nodded for him to continue.

"There's a wide stream that cuts across the plains near our farm. It wouldn't be too hard to divert that stream into the trench and fill it with water. That would make it even harder for animals to cross. We would have to make sure there weren't any trees around because monkeys are clever enough to break off branches and float across the water on them," Ibrahim concluded.

Dr. Ngwari said, "Your plan probably won't cost too much money, and I think it will stop the wild beasts. You're probably in a hurry to do it, aren't you?"

"Yes, the animals are destroying our vines and we won't have any grapes to sell unless we protect them," Ibrahim said.

The professor looked at Mr. Ngobe and grinned. "Would you like to enroll your son right now, or are you going to wait until there's nothing left we can teach him?"

Mr. Ngobe laughed. "It looks as if I should spend a little

more time talking to my son, doesn't it? I might learn a few things too."

The men stood and shook hands. The professor said, "I think Ibrahim's ideas will work. I'll talk with the other professors and I'll round up some student labor. I'll also talk with the head of the Program of Assistance for the Protection of Wild Animals about lending you an earth-mover and a man to operate it. I'm sure he'll be interested in helping you."

"We'll talk with our neighbors and find out how much equipment and labor they can spare," Mr. Ngobe said. "Thanks for meeting with us. We'd like to invite you to come to the farm sometime and stay for supper. My wife is the best cook in the highlands."

"You can count on me. Ibrahim, it was a pleasure meeting you. I'll see you at your farm, and you can introduce me to your zoo," the professor said.

Because Ibrahim had never before been to either the college or the city, his father showed him all the interesting sights before they started the trip home.

On the road, up and down the hills and valleys, Mr. Ngobe drove in silence as he thought about the plan for digging the trench. Ibrahim was deep in his own thoughts.

Finally, Mr. Ngobe turned to Ibrahim and said, "Well, Ibrahim, school starts next week. Did you enjoy your vacation? Are you sorry it's over?"

Ibrahim thought about it for a minute. "I've been thinking about that, Dad. I thought I wanted to get out of the vineyard and stop worrying about the grape crop, but I guess I'm going to miss it. I'm going to miss the baby giraffe and zebra, and the monkey that stole my waterbag. Dad, if we dig a trench the animals can't cross, I won't have any animals to talk to anymore. Do you think I can have a pet now?"

Mr. Ngobe smiled. "Yes, I think you can. How about a chicken or a goat you can feed every night?" he asked.

"Oh, Dad—" Ibrahim started to object until he noticed a big grin on his father's face and realized he was teasing.

"Right!" Ibrahim said. "That's exactly what I want. Chickens and goats to feed every night, and a wet puddle of mud."

"We'll get to work on that puddle as soon as we get home," Mr. Ngobe said. "If the silky, black-and-white pet monkey that's waiting for you at home finds the puddle and wants to play, I guess you'll just have to make sure it has someone to play with, won't you?"

"Thanks, Dad!" Ibrahim said with excitement.

"Ibrahim, I've been watching you closely, and I believe you're ready for more responsibility. I'm giving you the casava melon field in addition to the vineyard to take care of. I'll assign two workers to help you. You'll be the foreman for the entire north side of the farm."

"Dad! Thank you! That's what I've always dreamed of! I promise I'll pay attention to my work and I'll do the best job I can," Ibrahim said.

"Your mother and I think you have earned a reward, especially since we didn't believe you when you told us about the hippos. I should have looked for tracks and damage the first time it happened, but my mind was on the other crops and workers. I apologize for not having confidence in you."

Ibrahim's father had never before talked to him as if he were an adult. The boy hardly knew what to say.

"Your mother and I decided that we're going to take you more seriously. The first thing we're going to do is hire your uncle who runs in the Olympics to train you to race. We talked to him a few days ago, and he believes you have the ability and the drive to be an outstanding runner. He'll come on Sunday to work out a training schedule. How does that sound?"

Ibrahim was so happy and excited that he bounced up and down on the seat, raising his clenched fists over his head in a victory gesture. He imagined he heard an Olympic crowd cheering him as he raced to the finish line.

"Dad, thank you for giving me the chance to become a runner. I'll try to make you and Mother proud!"

CHAPTER FOURTEEN

You'll Be Proud
of Both of Us

ON A SATURDAY, a few weeks after the grapes had been harvested and sold, Ibrahim and Jaroni were sitting on the fence watching the Colobus monkey play with the goats. They heard a motor and looked up. A shiny car with the emblem of the agricultural college on the door stopped in front of their house.

Ibrahim shouted, "Dr. Ngwari! Hello!" He and Jaroni jumped down and ran to shake the professor's hand.

"Hello. I hear we solved the problem of the animal invaders in time to save your grapes. Is that true?" the professor asked.

"Yes, thanks for helping us so much."

"Is your father . . . Ah, Mr. Ngobe! How nice to see you."

"It's a pleasure to see you, Dr. Ngwari. Come in and meet my wife. She's heard all about you."

They went into the kitchen where Mrs. Ngobe was preparing supper. The professor inhaled the wonderful aroma of

freshly baked bread and said, "Mrs. Ngobe, your bread smells good enough for the gods."

Mrs. Ngobe smiled. "Thank you. Won't you stay and eat with us?"

"Yes, if it's not too much trouble. I'd like that very much. Actually, I must confess that that's one of the reasons I'm here. I couldn't forget your husband's invitation."

The men and children sat down at the table, and Mrs. Ngobe brought bowls, trays, and baskets of delicious food.

"The other reason I came here today is to present an award to Ibrahim. The Dean of Animal Husbandry proposed to the president of the college that we present a full scholarship to your son. The faculty voted in favor of it unanimously. We want to make sure our college is the one this young man attends."

Mrs. Ngobe, absolutely surprised, caught her breath.

Mr. Ngobe beamed. He stood up, shook Dr. Ngwari's hand, and said, "Please express our appreciation to the president, the dean, and the faculty. We are very grateful."

The children watched with big eyes and smiles, knowing something good was happening—even if they didn't understand it.

Ibrahim walked around the table, shook Dr. Ngwari's hand, and said, "Thank you, sir. You helped us save our grape crop, and now you're guaranteeing that I can go to your college. I'll try to live up to your expectations and make you proud."

Little Wanjiri hopped off her chair, went around the table and climbed up into Dr. Ngwari's lap. She patted his shoulder with her pineapple-sticky hands, and smacked his cheek with a wet kiss. "Thank you, Dr. Ngwari. I'm going to college with Ibrahim. You'll be proud of both of us, won't you?"